CROSBY AND ME

written by
Hugh MacDonald

illustrated by
Dale McNevin

The Acorn Press
Charlottetown
2010

acornpresscanada.com
P.O. Box 22024
Charlottetown, Prince Edward Island
C1A 9J2

Printed and bound in Canada
Cover and interior design by Matt Reid

Library and Archives Canada Cataloguing in Publication

MacDonald, Hugh, 1945-
Crosby and me / Hugh MacDonald, Dale McNevin.
ISBN 978-1-894838-50-4

I. McNevin, Dale, 1945- II. Title.
PS8575.D6306C76 2010   jC813'.54   C2010-905346-X

The publisher acknowledges the support of the Government of Canada through the Canada Book Fund of the Department of Canadian Heritage and the Canada Council for the Arts Block Grant Program.

Mixed Sources
Cert no. SW-COC-001271
© 1996 FSC

FSC

For our granddogs, Fozzie, Cocoa,
Moulin, Hazey, K.C., and Beacon
-HM

For Will and Kate
-DM

I'm off to play hockey
but I'm starting to think
dad's dreams are the reason
we go to the rink.

He's doing the driving with
Mum at his side;
our frisky dog Crosby comes
along for the ride.

And dad is reminding me
how I ought to play.
He says the same things
almost every day

My mom sits knitting
my new hockey sweater
while my dad raves on
about how to play better.

Before we leave home
I check on my gear.
I glance in the bag,
say, "I think it's all here."

So when we arrive,
I hurry right in.
I'll put on my gear
so the game can begin.

I pull on my cup,
get my garter belt on,
tape up my shin pads
till the tape is near gone.

Put on the worn stockings
that used to be Dad's,
hockey pants, neck guard,
elbow pads, shoulder pads.

Mom finished my sweater,
Dad says it looks great.
But then I discover…
I'm missing one skate.

My father is flustered,
he's beginning to pout.
He looks through the bag,
tosses all my things out.

He looks and he looks
still hoping to find it.
There's one glove in there,
he even glances inside it.

All the rest of my team file out of the room.

I sit with my dad in the dressing room gloom.

He looks at his watch,
It's now time for the game.
Half an hour to home.
the drive back takes the same.

The whole thing will be over
by the time he gets back.
His eyebrows look stormy,
all bushy and black.

His forehead is wrinkled,
he's rubbing his neck.
He glares and he sighs,
"I told you to check."

Just at that moment
Mom comes through the door.
Dad says, "How many times
have I told you before.

We're all really sorry
but this won't work, I think.
So let's head for home,
get away from this rink."

But Mom just stands there
with one of those faces,
and says, "It was you
who put in his new laces?"

Then Dad drops his jaw,
has a deep furrowed brow.
He looks like a drift
in the path of a plow.

He lowers his head
and he lets out a groan.
"I set one skate down
when I answered the phone."

So I take my gear off
and we start to head out,
but as we get to the door
I hear someone shout.

"I'll lend you my skates.
I'm done for the day.
So if they're your size,
you can still get to play."

It is Suzy McGregor,
which suits me just fine,
as long as her feet
are the same size as mine.

With Crosby beside me
I tie those skates tight
and burst out on the ice
like a jet taking flight.

I hear my dad cheering.
I tweak the twines twice
and Crosby goes crazy
like a cat chasing mice.

So everyone's happy
as we pull into our lane.
Gone is the tension,
the stress and the strain.

Father is cheerful
recalling my goals.
Crosby is thinking
of dog treats in bowls.

Mother is happy,
my new sweater fits right.
And I have decided
tonight is the night.

I say it out loud
for my father to hear,
"There's worse things in life
than forgetting some gear.

"So I'll keep playing hockey
so long as it's fun.
And it's nice if you watch me
just 'cause I'm your son.

"But if it makes us unhappy,
and we all get too tense,
then I don't want to play,
it doesn't make sense."

My dad nods his head
and so does my mother.
We do a group hug
'cause we love one another.

We order a pizza
since we all agree,
my mom and my dad
and Crosby and me.